PAPERCUTZ™

Geronimo Stilton

GRAPHIC NOVELS AVAILABLE FROM PAPERCUTZ

#1
"The Discovery of America"

#2
"The Secret of the Sphinx"

#3
"The Coliseum Con"

#4
"Following the Trail of Marco Polo"

#5
"The Great Ice Age"

#6
"Who Stole The Mona Lisa?"

#7
"Dinosaurs in Action"

#8
"Play It Again, Mozart!"

#9
"The Weird Book Machine"

#10
"Geronimo Stilton Saves the Olympics"

#11
"We'll Always Have Paris"

#12
"The First Samurai"

#13
"The Fastest Train in the West"

#14
"The First Mouse on the Moon"

#15
"All for Stilton, Stilton for All!"

#16
"Lights, Camera, Stilton!"

#17
"The Mystery of the Pirate Ship"

#18
"First to the Last Place on Earth"

#19
"Lost in Translation"

GERONIMO STILTON REPORTER #1
"Operation ShuFongfong"

GERONIMO STILTON REPORTER #2
"It's My Scoop"

GERONIMO STILTON REPORTER #3
"Stop Acting Around"

GERONIMO STILTON REPORTER #4
"The Mummy with No Name"

GERONIMO STILTON REPORTER #5
"Barry the Moustache"

GERONIMO STILTON REPORTER #6
"Paws Off, Cheddarface!"

GERONIMO STILTON REPORTER #8
"Hypno-Tick Tock"

GERONIMO STILTON REPORTER #9
"Mask of the Rat-Jitsu"

GERONIMO STILTON 3 in 1 #1

GERONIMO STILTON 3 in 1 #2

GERONIMO STILTON 3 in 1 #3

...ALSO AVAILABLE WHEREVER E-BOOKS ARE SOLD!

See more at papercutz.com

#10 BLACKRAT'S TREASURE

By Geronimo Stilton

NEW YORK

BLACKRAT'S TREASURE

Text by GERONIMO STILTON
Cover by ALESSANDRO MUSCILLO (artist) and CHRISTIAN ALIPRANDI (colorist)
Editorial supervision by ALESSANDRA BERELLO (Atlantyca S.p.A.)
Editing by ANITA DENTI (Atlantyca S.p.A.)
Script by DARIO SICCHIO
Art by ALESSANDRO MUSCILLO
Color by CHRISTIAN ALIPRANDI
Original Lettering by MARIA LETIZIA MIRABELLA

Special thanks to CARMEN CASTILLO

Based on an original idea by ELISABETTA DAMI.
Based on episode 10 of the Geronimo Stilton animated series *"Il tesoro di Baffonero,"* ("Blackrat's Treasure") written by DIANE MOREL,
storyboard by RICCARDO AUDISIO
Preview based on episode 11 of the Geronimo Stilton animated series *"Mistero sul Roditore Express,"* ("Intrigue on the Rodent Express")
written by EARL KRESS, storyboard by PIER DI GIÀ & LISA ARIOLI
www.geronimostilton.com

JAYJAY JACKSON — Production
WILSON RAMOS JR. — Lettering
JEFF WHITMAN — Managing Editor
LILY LU — Editorial Intern
JIM SALICRUP
Editor-in-Chief

ISBN: 978-1-5458-0866-5

Printed in China
March 2022

Papercutz books may be purchased for business or promotional use.
For information on bulk purchases please contact
Macmillan Corporate and Premium Sales
Department at (800) 221-7945 x5442.

Distributed by Macmillan
First Papercutz Printing

NEW MOUSE CITY...
AT THE OFFICE OF Geronimo Stilton, EDITOR-IN-CHIEF OF THE RODENT'S GAZETTE...
...YES, YOU KNOW WHAT? MOVE THE "PEA-SOUP FOG HITS NEW MOUSE CITY" PIECE ONTO THE FRONT PAGE.
AND PUSH THE "UPCOMING MOUSE MUSICAL" BACK TO PAGE NINE.
AH, DELICIOUS!
AH, NO, NO, NOT YOU! SORRY. KEEP ME IN THE LOOP!

NOW, WHERE DID I PUT MY NOTES ON THIS SO-CALLED "BRIE-SMELLING THREE-HEADED MONSTER" THEA TOLD ME ABOUT...? IT'S SUPPOSED TO LIVE ON THE DOCKS. ANOTHER FAKE MONSTER STORY.
WHAT'S THAT? OH! MY UNFINISHED ARTICLE ON THIS INCREDIBLE BREAKTHROUGH IN CHEESE SLICING TECHNOLOGY... I SHOULD HAVE SENT IT THREE DAYS AGO...
TOO MUCH IS TOO MUCH, CUZ! YOU NEED A BREAK OR YOU WILL BREAK!
UNCLE G LOVES BEING BUSY. HOLIDAYS ARE POINTLESS TO HIM. UNLESS YOU GIVE HIM A SCOOP, HE WON'T BUDGE!
SLAM
GERONIMO! A WITNESS HAS SEEN IT ON THE DOCKS! AGAIN!
AH, FINE, THEA, FINE...

I'LL GO TO THE DOCKS, BUT ONLY TO PROVE THERE'S **NO MONSTER!**
I'LL BE RIGHT BACK!
WHERE'S HE GOING WITH THAT?!
YEAH, **RIGHT.** HE'S NOT STRESSED.
NEW MOUSE CITY DOCKS...

THEA! WHAT WAS I THINKING? IT'S COLD, IT'S DAMP, AND I CAN'T SEE A THING!
DON'T WORRY. IT'S SUPPOSED TO SMELL LIKE ROTTEN BRIE. THAT'S HOW WE'LL KNOW WHEN IT'S NEAR.
YOU KNOW I DON'T BELIEVE IN MONSTERS, THEA. ESPECIALLY NOT ONES THAT STINK LIKE ROTTEN CHEESE.
I'M GOING BACK!
!
AAAAAAH!
WE SAW IT! WE SAW IT!
YEAH, CAN YOU SMELL IT, UNCLE G?!

SNIFF
SNIFF
I... I... I DON'T SMELL A THING!
I'M GOING BACK FOR A NICE CUP OF TEA WHERE IT'S WARM...
PLUS I'VE GOT A LOT OF WORK TO DO.
UM, UNCLE GERONIMO?
GASP!
I'VE NEVER SEEN THIS HERE BEFORE!

ACCORDING TO MY BENPAD, THIS DOCK SPACE SHOULD BE VACANT.
THEN WHAT'S THIS SHIP DOING HERE?
WELL! LET'S GO TAKE A LOOK!
UH...
OH, I KNOW YOU HAVE A LOT OF WORK TO DO...
AH, BUT--
DON'T WORRY, CUZ. WE'LL LET YOU KNOW IF WE FIND ANYTHING.
UH, BUT...
GEE, I WONDER IF SALLY RATMOUSEN KNOWS ABOUT THIS. THIS COULD BE A BIG SCOOP FOR THE DAILY RAT...

FINE, FINE! ***I'M*** GOING TO CHECK AROUND. MY WORK CAN WAIT A BIT LONGER.
THAT'S ODD. THIS SHIP APPEARS TO BE AN AUTHENTIC ***PIRATE SHIP.***
WHERE IS EVERYONE?
MAYBE A THREE-HEADED MONSTER ATE EVERYONE.
THERE'S NO THREE-HEADED MONSTER, ***TRAP***. I'LL PROVE IT.
UH... HELLO?

OH!

HELLO. YOU MUST BE THE CAPTAIN.
MAYBE HE DIDN'T HEAR YOU? HE SAID...

YOU MUST BE THE CAPTAIN!

PARDON US. I'M GERONIMO STILTON, AND WITH ME ARE MY--

CREEEAAAK
AAAAAH!
SKLUNK
SPLOSH
FWOSH
FRUP
SPLASH

WHAT'S GOING ON?
WE'RE TRAPPED LIKE RATS!
DON'T LOOK NOW, UNCLE G, BUT THIS SHIP'S LEAVING PORT.
I AM NO RAT! I'M SURE THERE'S A LOGICAL EXPLANATION FOR WHAT'S GOING ON.
HAVE YOU NOTICED WE'RE THE ONLY ONES ON BOARD? HOW LOGICAL IS THAT?
TAP
KLUNK
TAP
KLUNK
TAP
KLUNK
!
!
!
!

IT COULDN'T BE...
WHERE ARE YOU GOING?
I LIKED IT BETTER WHEN WE WERE THE ONLY ONES HERE.
KREEEK
WHAT "COULDN'T IT BE"?
AH-HA! I KNEW IT! THE **BRINEY-BONES!** IT'S THE DREADED **CAPTAIN BLACKRAT'S** VESSEL.

BUT THAT'S IMPOSSIBLE! THE BRINEY-BONES WAS LOST AT SEA NEARLY THREE HUNDRED YEARS AGO.
HE GOT THE NAME BECAUSE HE WAS THE MEANEST RAT TO EVER SAIL THE SEVEN SEAS?
AND HE HAD A CRAB ON HIS SHOULDER?
AND A MEAN LOOK IN HIS ONE GOOD EYE?
WELL, I'LL BRIE! I DIDN'T REALIZE YOU WERE ALL SO GOOD AT PIRATE HISTORY.
THEY'RE NOT.
?!
I'M STANDIN' RIGHT HERE...

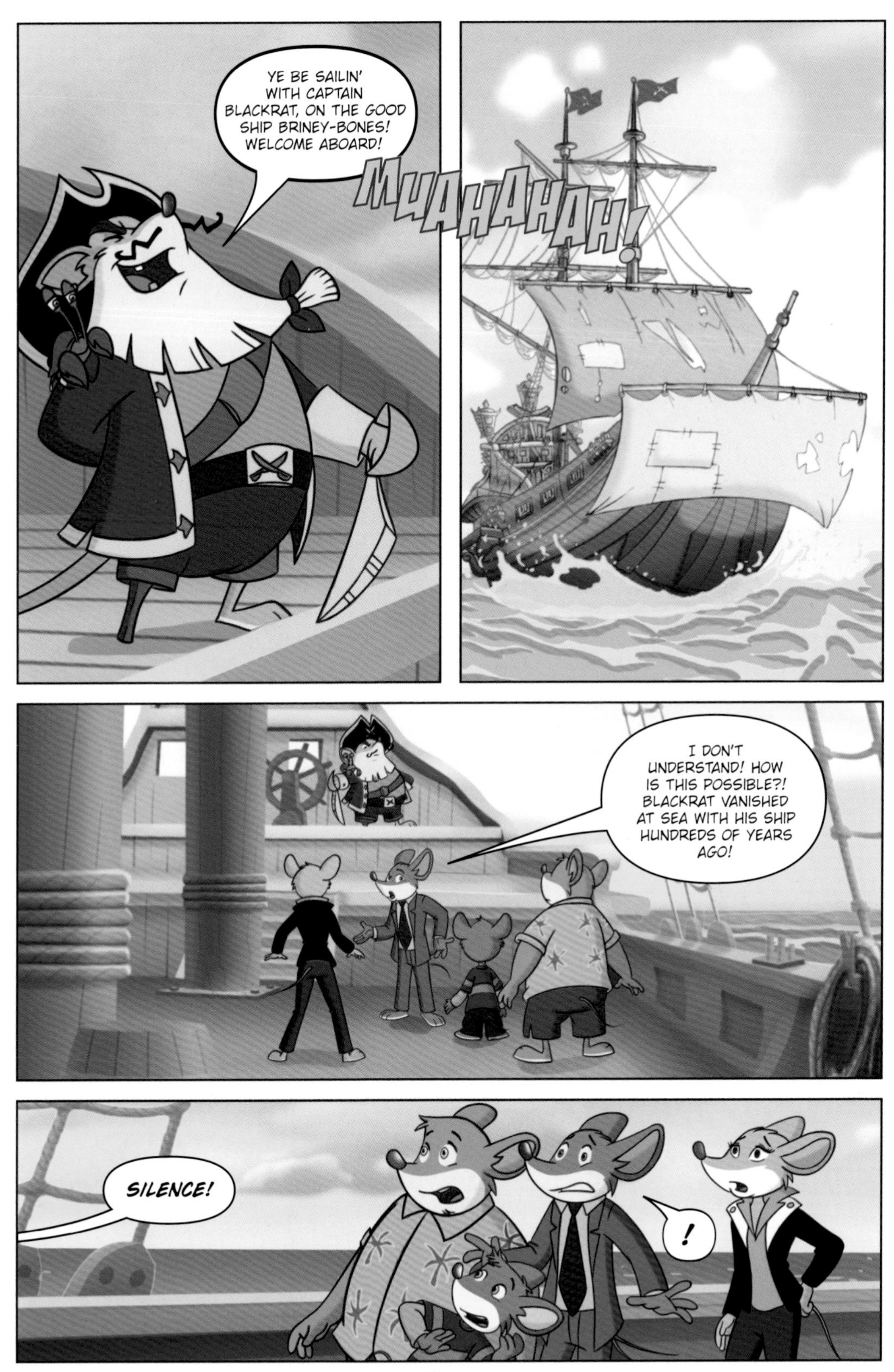
YE BE SAILIN' WITH CAPTAIN BLACKRAT, ON THE GOOD SHIP BRINEY-BONES! WELCOME ABOARD!
MUAHAHAHAH!
I DON'T UNDERSTAND! HOW IS THIS POSSIBLE?! BLACKRAT VANISHED AT SEA WITH HIS SHIP HUNDREDS OF YEARS AGO!
SILENCE!
!

SNIP
SNIP
ONLY SPEAK WHEN CAPTAIN BLACKRAT TELLS YOU SO!
U-UM, UH...
CAPTAIN... BLACKRAT? EXCUSE ME, BUT WHERE EXACTLY ARE WE GOING?
GOOD QUESTION! LOOK AROUND. WHAT DO YOU SEE?
A... DIRTY DECK?
BINGO, LADDY! SAY, SALTY, THIS YOUNG SWAB IS MIGHTY CLEVER. WHAT BE HIS NAME?!
BENJAMIN STILTON, CAPTAIN!

AYE, BENJAMIN. AS YE POINTED OUT, WE HAVE A DIRTY DECK AND A CREW OF FOUR!
NOW, GET TO WORK! I WANT TO SEE THIS BRIDGE SHINE!
"CREW"?
I'M **NOT** SCRUBBING ANY DECK!
AYE, YOU GOT SPIRIT! I LIKE THAT IN A CREWMAN--ER, WOMAN. ER, ***CREWPERSON***.
UH, MISTER CAPTAIN, SIR? BEFORE WE START SCRUBBING... COULD WE MAYBE HAVE LUNCH?
YOU WANT TO EAT? YOU WANT TO SLEEP? YER GOING TO SCRUB!
AND WHAT IF WE REFUSE?!
THEN IT'S THE PLANK AND ***DAVY JONES'S*** LOCKER! NOW, START SCRUBBIN'!

SOON AFTER...
SNIP
SNIP
SNIP
CAPTAIN, LOOK! BAD WEATHER AHEAD!
AYE, THAT JUST BE A SPRINKLE!
SO, CAPTAIN, WHAT HAPPENED TO YOUR LAST CREW?
-SIGH...- THE POOR SOULS WERE ALL LOST AT SEA ON ME LAST VOYAGE...

KRA-KOOM
-GULP!- C-CAPTAIN? THE SHIP'S STARTING TO ROCK A LOT!
TUMP
AAAH!
GERONIMO!
USE THE ROPE!

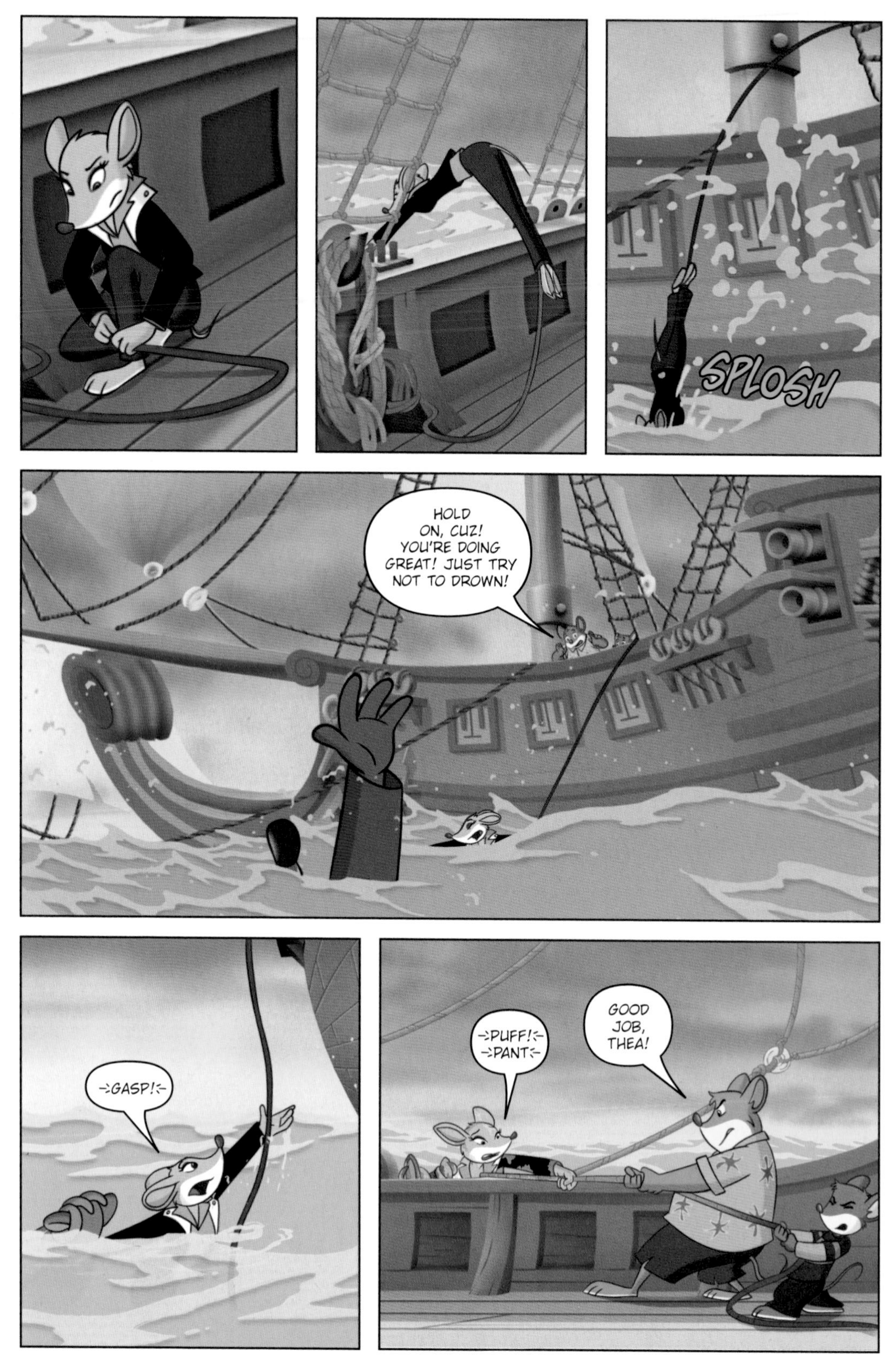
SPLOSH
HOLD ON, CUZ! YOU'RE DOING GREAT! JUST TRY NOT TO DROWN!
-GASP!-
-PUFF! -PANT-
GOOD JOB, THEA!

GNNN...
POP
SPUT... SPUT... OKAY, LOOK. I REALLY JUST WANT TO GO HOME...
I HAVE PLENTY OF WORK TO DO!
DO I HEAR SOMEONE COMPLAININ'?!
O-OH, NO! N-NOT AT ALL!
EVERYONE TO THEIR QUARTERS! ENOUGH WORK FOR TODAY!

*SEE ANY VOLUME OF ***GERONIMO STILTON*** GRAPHIC NOVELS FOR THOSE FEARSOME FELINES!

DID YOU SAY "TREASURE"?!
NO, WE'RE NOT PIRATES, BENJAMIN. WE MUST TAKE CONTROL OF THE SHIP AND TURN BACK AS QUICKLY AS POSSIBLE!

HOW? WE DON'T EVEN KNOW WHERE WE ARE.
HEH. DON'T LOOK AT ME. I LOST SIGNAL HOURS AGO... LOOKS LIKE WE'RE LOST AT SEA.

YAAAAWN! THIS WHOLE "WORK" THING REALLY WEARS A PERSON OUT. WHY DON'T WE GET SOME SLEEP?

THAT DOESN'T SOUND LIKE A BAD IDEA... YAAAWN.
NO! WE HAVE TO ACT ***NOW!***

HOW CAN WE TRUST THIS CAPTAIN?! SO FAR, HE'S KIDNAPPED US, FORCED US TO BE HIS CREW, AND... WHAT REALLY HAPPENED TO HIS OLD CREW?! WE HAVE TO LEAVE NOW! WHO'S WITH ME?!

SIGH. OF COURSE.
ZZZ
ZZZZ
ZZZ

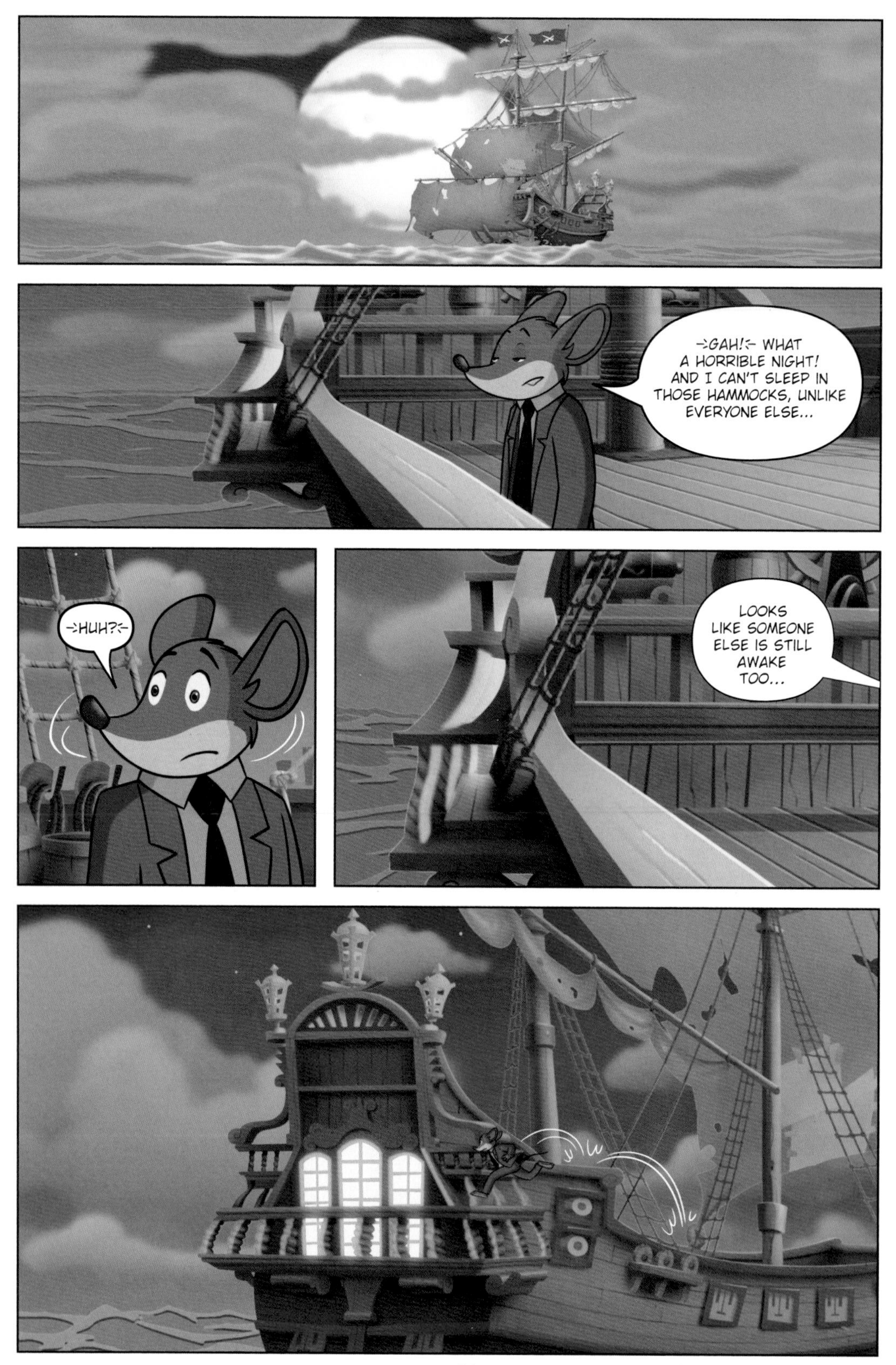
GAH! WHAT A HORRIBLE NIGHT! AND I CAN'T SLEEP IN THOSE HAMMOCKS, UNLIKE EVERYONE ELSE...
HUH?
LOOKS LIKE SOMEONE ELSE IS STILL AWAKE TOO...

?
HERE YE ARE, ME LOVELY. AT LAST, CRABCAKES, WITH THIS NEW CREW, THE TREASURE WILL BE MINE!
!
SNIP
OW! AH, RIGHT. I MEAN OURS!
THE TREASURE WILL BE OURS! HEHEHEHE...
DID HE SAY "TREASURE"?
BUMP
OW!
WHAT WAS THAT?!

BEST BE CAREFUL. NO TELLIN' WHO'S LURKIN' ABOUT AND LISTENIN'. NOW, WHERE WERE WE?
PSSSST
PSSST
OH, RIGHT, THE CREW! EXPENDABLE, AS USUAL! **AHAHAHAHAHA!**
AHAHAHAH
GULP!
DID HE JUST CALL THE CREW "EXPENDABLE"?!
HE WAS TALKING ABOUT A TREASURE MAP?! AWESOME!
WE'RE GOING ON A TREASURE HUNT!
DID YOU HEAR THE PART WHERE WE'RE ALL EXPENDABLE?
OH, UM... I DON'T WANT TO GO ANYMORE...

WHOA, WHOA, WHOA. OLD LICORICE TEETH EXPECTS US TO DO ALL THE WORK AND THEN... MAN! THIS GUY IS SUCH A... A...
PIRATE?
YEAH! YOU SAID IT.
IGNORING THE FACT THAT ONLY I SEEM TO CARE THAT WE'RE "EXPENDABLE," IF WE HAD THE MAP AND NOT HIM, THEN WE WOULD BE IN CONTROL.
BLACKRAT WILL ***HAVE*** TO LISTEN TO US!
I HAVE A PLAN, BUT WE'LL HAVE TO WAIT FOR SUN UP.
NOW, LISTEN CAREFULLY...

AYE, CRABCAKES.
IT BE A GRAND MORNIN' FOR HUNTIN' TREASURE! WHAT SAY YE?!
!
NO, WE'VE BEEN THROUGH THIS. YE CAN'T STEER THIS SHIP, YE SALTY-LIVERED CRUSTACEAN!
SNIP
SNIP
SNIP
SIGH
SOB
NOW, NOW. DON'T POUT. MAYBE LATER, I'LL LET YOU TAKE THE WHEEL.
YES, NOW THERE BE A GOOD BOY.
MORNING, CAPTAIN BLACKRAT!
YARR! YOU'RE UP EARLY!

WELL, WE WERE WONDERING IF YOU COULD TEACH US SOME MORE NIFTY PIRATE STUFF?
WHAT SORT OF STUFF?
OH, THE USUAL... PLUNDERING, PILLAGING, SQUANDERING...
ER, MISS. SQUANDERIN'S MORE A VIKING'S LINE OF WORK, NOT A PIRATE!
GAH! THAT MAP HAS TO BE SOMEWHERE!
IT'S JUST SOCKS... MORE SOCKS... SOCKS WITH HOLES... SOCKS WITH POLKA DOTS...
AND THIS ONE'S JUST HOLES...
PIRATE CAPTAINS DIDN'T HAVE SAFES IN THEIR QUARTERS. MAYBE THE DESK...

OH!
THERE IT IS!
SUCCULENT SWISS! GOT IT!
!
AND I GOT YOU!
YEAH, HE FIGURED OUT IT WAS A TRICK...
THAT'S BECAUSE SOMEONE WANTED TO LEARN HOW TO "DANCE LIKE A PIRATE."
LEPRECHAUNS DANCE! PIRATES DON'T! NOW, HAND OVER THE MAP! I KNOW HOW TO DEAL WITH A MUTINOUS CREW...

UH-UM! MAYBE WE COULD TALK ABOUT THIS...? SIT DOWN OVER A NICE CUP OF TEA? HAVE SOME CHEESE PERHAPS?
TRYIN' TO BRIBE THE CAPTAIN WITH TEA AND CHEESE, ARE YE?!
NO, NO, NO! GULP! HELP!
YOU CAN'T DO THIS!
I SWALLOWED A BUG!
LET HIM GO!
NO USE ARGUIN' IT! ME MIND'S MADE UP! IT'S THE BRINY DEEP FOR THE LOT OF YA!
GULP!

GNNNN!
STOP! THINK ABOUT WHAT YOU'RE DOING! YOU MAKE US ALL WALK THE PLANK, YOU WON'T HAVE A CREW!
AYE, I'M LISTENING...
WITHOUT A CREW, WHO'S GOING TO HELP YOU FIND THE TREASURE?
AYE, THE LAD SPEAKS TRUE... GOOD POINT.
WELL, COME ON, SALTY. DON'T JUST STAND THERE. DON'T WANT THE SHARKS TO NIP YE, EH?
YER FREE TO GO, BUT DON'T GO TOUCHIN' ME MAP AGAIN OR--
"IT'S THE BRINY DEEP." WE KNOW.
SNIP
SNIP
SNIP

RRRUUMBLE
KRA-KOOM
IT BE A FOUL NOR-EASTER MOVIN' IN...
ALL HANDS ON DECK!
SPLOSH
AHHHHH!

BLACKRAT! WE'VE GOT TO HELP HIM! QUICK! WE CAN'T LEAVE HIM!
I'M WITH YOU! COME ON, BENJAMIN!
TLAC
-GAH!- I'LL BE THERE IN A MINUTE!
FASTER! FASTER!
ROLL
ROLL
STUMP
AAAAAH!

YOU ALRIGHT, UNCLE G?
I'M ALRIGHT! I'M ALRIGHT! I LUCKILY FELL INTO THE LIFEBOAT...
AHOY, MATEY! GIVE ME A HAND?!
SPLOSH
AAAAH!
YA DID IT, SALTY! YER A TRUE PIRATE HERO! YA SAVED ME AND CRABCAKES FROM THE--
AAAAAH! CRABCAKES!

KRA-KOOM
HOLD ON, THE STORM'S GETTING WORSE!
NOOOO!
RRRUUMBLE
NOOOOOO!

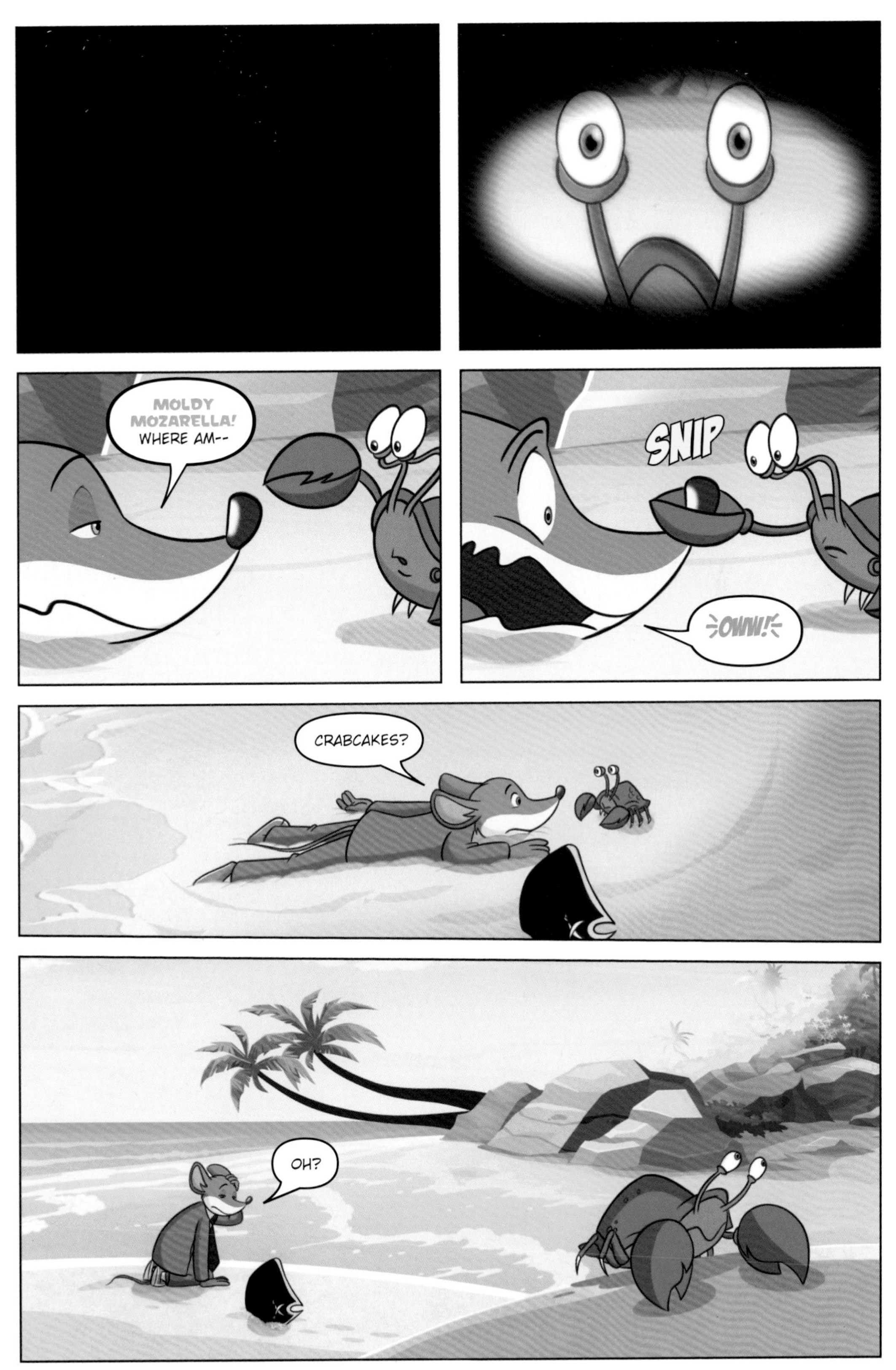
MOLDY MOZARELLA! WHERE AM--
SNIP
OWW!
CRABCAKES?
OH?

HOW ARE YOU FEELING, UNCLE G?
GOOD MORNING!
I'M FEELING BETTER BUT... WHERE ARE WE?
WE LANDED IN PARADISE, CUZ! LOOK AROUND!
WHAT HAPPENED?
THE STORM WASHED US ALL OVERBOARD AND WE ENDED UP HERE.
RIGHT WHERE WE WANT TO BE... ***THE ISLAND OF MALA SUERTE!***
THIS IS WHERE THE TREASURE BE!
REALLY?! THAT MEANS WE CAN--
HUNT FOR TREASURE!

LATER...
WAIT HERE, ME HEARTIES. I'LL GIVE A LOOK AROUND!
KAW
KAW
KAW
AAAAH!
CALM DOWN. CHANCES ARE, WHATEVER'S OUT THERE IS MORE AFRAID OF YOU THAN YOU ARE OF IT. YOU KNOW?
GERONIMO?
GERONIMO!
OH, NO! HE'S GONE! THIS ISLAND IS CURSED! HELP!
LET'S LOOK FOR HIM. I'M SURE HE'S CLOSE.

HM?
FRUSH

AAAH! HIS HAT?! OH, NO! HE'S FALLEN INTO QUICKSAND!

HEY, WAIT, THIS ISN'T QUICKSAND...
TAP
TAP
TAP

AAAAAH!
OOF!
SPLATT

YOU OKAY, BROTHER?
THOSE... THOSE MONKEYS TOOK MY CLOTHES!

HEE
HEE
HEE
HEE
HEE
HEE
HEE

AVAST! ME AND CRABCAKES FOUND A WAY TO THE TREASURE!

OH!

I SEE THE MONKEYS TOOK YER CLOTHES. SPITEFUL CREATURES THEY BE... NOW, FOLLOW ME!

UH... WHY DON'T YOU GO AHEAD? I'LL WAIT FOR YOU ALL BACK AT THE BEACH...
COME ON, UNCLE G. WE GOT THIS FAR!
AND YE GOIN' FARTHER, IF YE GET ME POINT!
GULP! G-GOT IT!
A-ACHOO! SORRY...

!
LOOK! IS THAT A--
TREASURE CHEST?
TREASURE IT BE, SAYS I! AT LAST! IT'S MINE! ALL MINE!
SNAP
AND CRABCAKES'S TOO!
MPF
YOURS?! AFTER ALL WE WENT THROUGH? YOU OWE US!
LIKE ANY PIRATE CREW!

YER RIGHT... YOU ALL DESERVE A CUT OF THE TREASURE. ESPECIALLY YOU, SALTY! YOU SAVED ME AND CRABCAKES!

I'LL EVEN GIVE YOU THE HONOR OF OPENIN' THE CHEST!
WHAT?

CAN I REALLY?
YE EARNED IT. BESIDES, THE MONKEYS STOLE YER CLOTHES AND I FEEL A LITTLE... SORRY FOR YA.

KLUNK

SPROING
AAAAAH!
HAHAHAHAHA!
I THINK THERE BE SOMETHIN' RICH ON THE CARD FOR YA!
"CONGRATULATIONS, GERONIMO, YOU'VE... WON..."? "YOU'VE FOUND THE TREASURE. WE HOPE YOU'VE ENJOYED YOUR PIRATE ADVENTURE CRUISE"?
"CRUISE"?! WHAT?
TIME TO SAY GOODBYE, SALTY! I HOPE YOU'VE HAD A GREAT VACATION WITH ME AND CRABCAKES HERE!

YOU'VE BEEN THE BEST CREW EVER! HAVE A SAFE TRIP HOME!
A SHUTTLE BOAT TO NEW MOUSE CITY'S WAITIN' FOR YA ON THE BEACH.
WHAT? HOW? THIS WAS A "VACATION"?!
WE HAD TO FIND SOME WAY TO GET YOU AWAY FROM WORK SO YOU COULD RELAX.
YOU MEAN IT WAS ALL JUST A CRUISE?
NONE OF IT WAS REAL?
WELL, THE STORM WAS REAL.
AND THE MONKEYS!

SO, YOU TRICKED ME?! I WAS SEASICK, NEARLY DROWNED, ATTACKED, TIED UP, AND SHIPWRECKED!
SO... ARE YOU UPSET?
I... I...
AHAHAHAHAHAH!
NO! THANK YOU SO MUCH! I JUST WISH I HADN'T WORN MY BEST SUIT!
LOOK AT IT THIS WAY... THERE'S SOME MONKEY OUT THERE WHO'S DRESSED WAY BETTER THAN THE OTHERS!
HEE HEE
HEE
HEE
HEE
HEE
HEE

I LEARNED A LOT ON MY VACATION.

REC
TOGETHER WITH MY FAMILY, WE LIVED AN EXCITING ADVENTURE AND HAD A LOT OF FUN!
EVEN IF WE HADN'T FOUND THE TREASURE, WHAT COUNTED WAS THAT WE SPENT THE TIME HELPING EACH OTHER. I LOOK FORWARD TO MANY MORE ADVENTURES WITH MY FAMILY.
00:30:07

FOR THE ***RODENT'S GAZETTE***, I'M GERONIMO STILTON! SEE YOU NEXT TIME!

URGENT PAPER DELIVERY, GERONIMO!
OH, NO! LOOK AT HOW MUCH WORK'S PILED UP WHILE I WAS GONE!
-SIGH.- IT'S EVEN WORSE THAN BEFORE!
JUST A REMINDER NOT TO WORK TOO HARD, OKAY?
-ARG!- DID I HEAR SOMEONE COMPLAININ', SAILOR?!
NO, NOT AT ALL, **CAPTAIN GERONIMO!**
-ARG!- THEN LET'S PRETEND WE STILL BE ON VACATION AND HAVE A YUMMY CRUSTY SAILOR SNACK DOWN AT THE PORT RESTAURANT!
AYE AYE, CAPTAIN!
HEY, WAIT FOR ME!

Watch Out For PAPERCUTZ™

Welcome to the timber-shivered tenth GERONIMO STILTON REPORTER graphic novel, “Blackrat’s Treasure,” the official comics adaptation of the animated Geronimo Stilton TV series, Season One, Episode 10, written by Diane Morel, brought to you by Papercutz—those salty landlubbers dedicated to publishing great graphic novels for all ages. I’m *Jim Salicrup*, the Editor-in-Chief and Crabcake’s personal valet, here to talk about a few other Papercutz books you’re likely to enjoy…

First off, there are the original GERONIMO STILTON graphic novels (see page 2), which feature Geronimo and his friends and relatives saving the future by protecting the past. That means that Geronimo and some combination of Trap, Benjamin, Thea, Bugsy Wugsy, or a special friend, literally journey back in time to keep the Pirate Cats (Catardone III of Catatonia, his daughter Tersilla, and their lackey, Bonzo) from tampering with time to selfishly benefit themselves in some grand wicked scheme. Fortunately, Geronimo’s good friend Professor Von Volt is able to track the time-travelling activities of the Pirate Cats with his high-tech Tempograph machine and then send Geronimo and his team to whatever time the Pirate Cats are at via the Speedrat—a super-cool time machine that he invented. Every time they go back in time, they wind up witnessing an important event in history, except it’s on their parallel mouse-world. So it’s mice versions of such historic figures as Christopher Columbus, Marco Polo, Leonardo DaVinci, Wolfgang Amadeus Mozart, and others that you wind up meeting, but oddly enough, all the basic facts presented about them are the same as the those regarding their human counterparts.

If for some crazy reason you’d prefer humans, as opposed to human-like mice, to take you through time, then I suggest another great Papercutz graphic novel series, MAGICAL HISTORY TOUR. This compact comic series features Annie and her brother Nico going back through time to explore such exciting topics as The Great Pyramid, The Great Wall of China, Hidden Oil, The Crusades and the Holy Wars, The Plague, Albert Einstein, Gandhi, Vikings, and more. It’s well researched by writer Fabrice Erre and beautifully illustrated by artist Sylvain Savoia. Co-Editor Lewis Trondheim says of editing the series that “it’s a great power to give young readers the keys to understanding our world. And this [MAGICAL HISTORY TOUR] does that, without lecturing too much, with a drop of humor, but remaining factual. It’s a very exciting challenge. Basically I try to be the teacher that I would have loved to have when I was 10.”

Magical History Tour ©2022 DUPUIS - Erre - Savoia

But if this is starting to sound too much like going to school, well, let me tell you that Papercutz features some of the coolest schools you’ve ever seen…

The GEEKY F@B 5 attend Earheart Elementary School, where four of the GEEKY F@B 5 attend the marvelous Miss Malone’s class. Lucy, Zara, A.J., and Sofia (along with Lucy’s older sister Marina, and their cat Hubble) use their brains to tackle all sorts of real-life problems and discover that when girls stick together anything is possible. GEEKY F@B 5 is written by mother/daughter team Liz and Lucy Lareau, and drawn by Ryan Jampole.

Meanwhile, older girls Julie, Lucie, and Alia enjoy learning about their passion in DANCE CLASS, a school that covers a wide range of dance—everything from Classical Ballet to Hip-Hop. Written by Béka and drawn by Crip, you’ll feel like you’re right there learning to dance, while getting to know almost every teacher, student, and even their friends and families.

We also have a couple of schools that are really out of this world—the SCHOOL FOR EXTRATERRESTRIAL GIRLS, where Tara Smith winds up after discovering everything she thought she knew about her life was a lie, including that she’s not even human. It’s an exciting Sci-Fi series written by Jeremy Whitley and drawn by Jamie Noguchi.

And there’s Destiny, the magical school flying unicorns attend in the graphic novel series MELOWY, written by Cortney Powell and drawn by Ryan Jampole. At Destiny, magical pegasuses called Melowies, born with symbols on their wings bestowing them with hidden powers, study to prepare for their true potential. This is where friends Cleo, Cora, Maya, Selena, and Electra form their special bond and face their destinies as Melowies.

Who knew schools could be so cool… and weird? A mouse editing a newspaper doesn’t seem that odd now, I bet! Speaking of news, wait’ll you see what’s waiting for you in the next volume of GERONIMO STILTON REPORTER. It’s a story called “Intrigue on the Rodent Express,” and you can check out the preview for it on the very next page! And the best part is, you don’t even need a train ticket to hop aboard!

Thanks,

STAY IN TOUCH!

EMAIL: salicrup@papercutz.com
WEB: papercutz.com
TWITTER: @papercutzgn
INSTAGRAM: @papercutzgn
FACEBOOK: PAPERCUTZGRAPHICNOVELS
SNAIL MAIL: Papercutz, 160 Broadway, Suite 700, East Wing, New York, NY 10038

Go to papercutz.com and sign up for the free Papercutz e-newsletter!

Special Preview of GERONIMO STILTON REPORTER Graphic Novel #11 "Intrigue on the Rodent Express"!

SBRAM
NOW, WE HAD BETTER GET PACKED AND READY FOR THE TRIP.
I'LL TEXT *THEA* TO BE READY TO FLY US THERE!
WE WON'T BE FLYING. THERE ARE NO LANDING STRIPS ON FROZEN FUR PEAK.
NO, WE'LL BE TRAVELLING IN A MORE ELEGANT AND DECIDEDLY SAFER MANNER...
ABOARD THE FAMOUS ***RODENT EXPRESS!***
AH, I LOVE TRAINS!

DID I HEAR SOMETHING ABOUT A TRIP?
AAAAAAAAAAH!
SWISSS
SBRANG
THANKS, TRAP.
EHEHEHEH... ARE YOU SURE TRAIN TRAVEL IS SAFER?

AH! NOW, THIS IS HOW MOUSE WAS MEANT TO TRAVEL!
THE BEAUTIFUL SCENERY PASSING BEFORE YOUR EYES, THE CALMING CLICKETY-CLACK OF THE RAILS. WOULDN'T YOU AGREE, BENJAMIN?

Don't Miss GERONIMO STILTON REPORTER #11
"Intrigue on the Rodent Express"! Coming soon!